Bad Business

Diane Dakers

Orca currents

ORCA BOOK PUBLISHERS

Copyright © 2015 Diane Dakers

All rights reserved. No part of this publication may be reproduced
or transmitted in any form or by any means, electronic or mechanical, including
photocopying, recording or by any information storage and retrieval system now
known or to be invented, without permission in writing from the publisher.

Library and Archives Canada Cataloguing in Publication

Dakers, Diane, author
Bad business / Diane Dakers.
(Orca currents)

Issued in print and electronic formats.
ISBN 978-1-4598-0969-7 (pbk.).—ISBN 978-1-4598-0971-0 (pdf).—
ISBN 978-1-4598-0972-7 (epub)

I. Title. II. Series: Orca currents
PS8607.A43B33 2015   jc813'.6   c2015-901706-8
                             c2015-901707-6

First published in the United States, 2015
Library of Congress Control Number: 2015935518

Summary: Lindy takes advantage of an elderly woman she works for.

MIX
Paper from
responsible sources
FSC® C016245
www.fsc.org

*Orca Book Publishers is dedicated to preserving the environment and has
printed this book on Forest Stewardship Council® certified paper.*

Orca Book Publishers gratefully acknowledges the support for its
publishing programs provided by the following agencies: the Government of
Canada through the Canada Book Fund and the Canada Council for the Arts,
and the Province of British Columbia through the BC Arts Council
and the Book Publishing Tax Credit.

Cover photography by Shutterstock.com
Author photo by Christine Tripp

ORCA BOOK PUBLISHERS
www.orcabook.com

Printed and bound in Canada.

18 17 16 15 • 4 3 2 1

*To Mom and Auntie J,
who inspired this story*

Chapter One

The kitchen is choked with smoke. The fire alarm is blaring. And the old lady is just standing there, clutching her oven mitts to her chest. "Mrs. Naulty," I scream at her. "What are you doing?"

She stares at the toaster oven, the source of the billowing smoke. I snatch the oven mitts from her and fling open the glass door. My eyes water from the stench of burning plastic. I can almost feel brain cells dying with every toxic breath I take.

I yank a smoldering frozen dinner out of the toaster oven and throw it in the sink. It's still in its plastic wrapper and cardboard box, frozen and charred at the same time.

I turn on the tap to douse the burning box. Mrs. Naulty starts whimpering. "I don't understand. I don't understand." *What's not to understand? You have to take the food out of the package before you cook it. It's pretty simple.*

I unplug the toaster oven and fan the smoke to clear the air. Mrs. Naulty covers her ears to block the screaming fire alarm. She closes her eyes tight and scrunches up her nose. But she can't escape the sight, sound and smell of her mistake.

Suddenly, I feel sad for her. I've known Mrs. Naulty for fifteen years—

my whole life. She's the neighborhood grandma. She invites us in for cookies after school and gives out supersized chocolate bars at Halloween. She's the little old lady who sits on the porch and waves to everyone who passes by.

At this moment, though, she's just a confused senior citizen. I'd never really noticed how old and wrinkly she's gotten. She must be about eighty-five. Her grandson Roger is practically old enough to be my father.

Right now, she reminds me of a scared puppy, like she knows she's in trouble for something, but she doesn't quite know what she's done wrong. She is so upset and confused that I can't be mad at her. Even though she almost burned down her house.

I take a breath and lead her into the living room. "Would you like a cup of tea, Mrs. Naulty?" I ask loudly. "Maybe a sandwich too?"

She nods. "That would be lovely, Lindy." I sit her down and return to the kitchen. I open a window to clear the air, willing the fire alarm to shut up.

Every Saturday, I help Mrs. Naulty around her house. She's one of my "clients," as I call the old people who pay me to do odd jobs. Mrs. Naulty is the only one I see every week. The others call when they have specific projects for me.

It's a sweet business. On a good day, I can make seventy dollars. And mostly it's fun. Some days I get to paint fences or put up Christmas decorations or trim hedges. Other days they're more boring jobs, like dusting, washing dishes or sweeping out a garage. I charge ten dollars an hour. Except for Mrs. Naulty. Every Saturday, no matter how much work I do for her, she gives me two five-dollar bills in a flowery pink envelope. I've been helping her out since I was little—back when two five-dollar bills were a big deal. Now it bugs me that she doesn't pay me enough for all the grief I put up with at her house. Like today's fire drill. Sometimes I think I should ditch her and find another regular client who will pay my full rate.

Finally, the fire alarm stops screeching. I throw the soggy frozen-dinner box into the garbage before I deliver a cheese-and-tomato sandwich and a cup of tea to the living room.

"Thank you, dear," says Mrs. Naulty. "Have you finished your chores for today? I baked cookies yesterday. They're in the tin on the counter. Why don't you help yourself and then come sit with me for a few minutes before you go home."

Sure. Because having a tea party with a little old lady is how I like to spend my Saturday afternoons. *Maybe instead of cookies, you should give me a tip for everything I do for you*, I want to scream at her.

But I guess cookies are better than nothing. And Mrs. Naulty's chocolate-chip-cranberry-orange ones are awesome. So okay, I'll sit down and have a cookie. Or two.

Chapter Two

The first thing I do when I get home every Saturday is count my money. I usually go straight to my room and double-check my take for the day. Then I update my Excel spreadsheet. That's where I keep track of how much money I have and how much I still need to earn for my Arctic trip.

Today, Mom has other plans for me. I'm barely through the door when she calls to me. "Lindy, is that you? Perfect timing! Could you come help me, please?"

Seriously? I haven't even taken my boots off yet. I've been working for crazy old people all day. I wouldn't mind a minute to breathe.

I stare at the ceiling for a couple of seconds. All I want to do is go to my room and update my spreadsheet.

"Lindy, are you there?"

Of course I'm here. I didn't vanish. "Coming," I yell as I untie my boots. I suppose it wouldn't kill me to see what she's doing.

I find her in her office on a ladder, a pencil in one hand, a framed picture in the other. "Hi, Lin. I bought this painting today. I love it, but I can't decide where to hang it. What do you think? Does it look good here?"

This is the big emergency? "Looks fine," I mumble.

"Or should it go farther to the right? I don't know. Help me move the ladder over, so I can show you what it looks like over there." We move the ladder. She shows me.

"I know you do this kind of thing for your clients all the time," she says. "It's good to have an expert in the family."

An expert. That makes me laugh. Mom is so dorky sometimes. But she actually seems to care what I think, so I decide that my spreadsheet can wait five minutes. "You know, Mom, I think the picture would look better on the wall beside the window. That way, you'll be able to see it as soon as you come into the room."

I show her what I mean.

"Huh," she says. "You're right. Good eye, girl!" She looks like she's about to high-five me, so I grab the pencil from her instead. She holds the painting while I mark an X on the wall where the nail will go.

"How was Mrs. Naulty today?" Mom asks as I hammer the nail in place.

"She's getting weirder every time I see her." I hand Mom the hammer. "Pass me the picture."

"What do you mean?"

I tell Mom about the fire alarm while I hang the picture and level it. "Lindy, that looks fantastic!" she interrupts. "I had no idea you were such a handywoman! I'm so impressed!"

Then you should give me two five-dollar bills in a flowery pink envelope, I joke to myself.

"That's so strange about Mrs. Naulty today," Mom says. "Imagine if you hadn't been there."

"I know. It was freaky. But it's not the first weird thing she's done. Last week, when she answered the door, she didn't even know who I was. I thought she was just messing with me. But then I realized she honestly didn't recognize me."

"Really, Lin? You didn't mention that."

"I guess I thought she was expecting someone else to be at the door. Or she was thinking about something else when I got there. I don't know. She remembered me pretty quick, so I forgot about it."

Then something else crosses my mind. "Mom, one day last month there was this man at Mrs. Naulty's when I got there. He had all these brochures and papers spread out on the table, and he was poking around under the kitchen sink."

I fold up the ladder. Mom puts the hammer and pencil back in the toolbox.

"Mrs. Naulty said she was buying a water filter from him. The guy was going to put it in for her right then and there."

I remember feeling totally creeped out for some reason.

"I thought it was weird because Roger installed a new water filter for her in January. I know because I helped him install it. I reminded her about that. I told her maybe she should talk to Roger before this guy installed anything."

"Did she call him?"

"I don't know. She didn't do it right then. The guy packed up his stuff and left. He said he would check back in a couple of days. I don't know if he did or not. I never asked."

"And today she put a frozen meal into the oven, plastic wrap and all," Mom says, like she's thinking out loud. "Thank goodness you were there, Lindy. Both times. Who knows how much money she would have given that crook?"

"I know, right? Maybe she's going a bit cuckoo." I circle my finger around the side of my head and cross my eyes. I laugh at my impression of a crazy person.

"Lindy, this could be serious," Mom says. "When people get old, they often start forgetting things. And Mrs. Naulty is, well, let me think, she must be eighty-seven or eighty-eight. She could be in the early stages of Alzheimer's or some other form of dementia."

That sounds bad. "Does that mean she'll have to go to a nursing home?" I ask. I don't want to get Mrs. N. in trouble. I don't want her to have to move out of her house because of me.

"I don't know, Lindy. But I am going to talk to Roger. He needs to know how confused his grandma is getting." Mom picks up the phone. "Thanks for helping with the picture," she calls to me as I head down the hall.

Finally, I can go to my room and update my spreadsheet. If I'm going to go to the Arctic this summer, I need to come up with $5,500 by the middle of March. Two weeks from now.

It's been my dream my whole life to see a polar bear. I have stuffed polar bears, polar-bear pj's, polar-bear wallpaper on my iPad and cell phone. I mean, I'm not dorky about it. I don't wear polar-bear T-shirts and earrings or anything like that. I just happen to love polar bears.

Then last year, in grade nine, I heard about this program called Students Up North—SUN for short. It's perfect. You get to go to the Arctic for two weeks with a bunch of kids from all over the world. It sounds amazing, though the website tries to make it sound like work: *This is not a vacation. This is an educational expedition.* Whatever. I don't care. I'm dying to go.

But they don't take just anybody. You have to be between fourteen and eighteen years old. You have to have good grades and be a total do-gooder at your school and in your community. You have to get reference letters and write an essay.

Mom and Dad said if I got accepted, I could go, but I'd have to pay for it myself. The full price of the trip is $10,000—and they don't have that kind of money lying around.

Last October, when I got the letter saying I'd been accepted into the program, I almost peed myself I was so excited. Nobody from my school has ever gone on a Students Up North trip. I will be the first. In history. That makes me sort of like an Arctic explorer.

The letter also said SUN was giving me a $2,500 scholarship to help pay for the trip. That means I only have to pay $7,500. And if I pay before the early-bird deadline, they'll knock another $2,000 off the price.

I figured I'd have no problem getting the cash together. I had a bit of money in the bank. I started working for the old people in the neighborhood last summer. I was sure I could earn what I needed.

What I didn't count on was winter. I had a couple of snow-shoveling jobs. And a few of my clients hired me around Christmastime to help with lights and decorations. But other than that, hardly any of them have called over the last five months.

Except Mrs. Naulty. Every Saturday like clockwork, I'm at her house. But her two measly five-dollar bills every week barely make a dent in the cost of my trip. I'm starting to panic that I won't make enough money in time.

Today's earnings aren't going to help me get there. I only made forty bucks. I add it to my spreadsheet and hit *Enter*.

The total is $4,975.

The early-bird deadline is in two weeks. There's no way I'm going to earn another $525 in time.

Chapter Three

Why is Shanna taking so long? We agreed to meet in the school library at three o'clock. I'm in the library. It's 3:20. And she's still not here.

I texted her five minutes ago, but she hasn't messaged me back.

I'm only going to wait ten more minutes. I google *Arctic charities* while I wait.

Finally, Shanna wanders into the library. She plunks herself down at the computer beside me.

"Where have you been?" I'm a bit annoyed, since the only reason I'm here is to help her with her Northern Discovery Club project.

"I'm not *that* late," Shanna says. She hands me a package of M&M's— even though there's no food allowed in the library. "I stopped to get you a little treat."

"Thanks," I say. "I'll save them for later."

"Have you found any good websites?" she asks, firing up the computer beside me.

I've only known Shanna since September, when she transferred to my school. She sat beside me at Northern Discovery Club, and we've been friends ever since. It's not like we hang out every day or anything, but I walk partway home with her after club meetings. And we usually work together on projects.

The Northern Discovery Club is for students who want to learn about Canada's Arctic. We learn about the wildlife, the people, the impacts of climate change. Everything.

Our homework from last month's meeting was to find an Arctic charity to support. On Monday, we're all going to make presentations about the charities we've chosen. The club will fundraise for only one project. After the presentations, we're going to vote on which to choose.

I have a huge list of options on my screen. "What kind of charity are you looking for, Shanna?" I ask. "Are you interested in animals? Or environmental groups? Or causes that help kids? Or old people?"

"I don't care," says Shanna. "Something that has a good website with lots of information I can present."

"Are you finding any charities you like?" I peek at her computer. She's on Facebook. "What are you doing?"

"Ummm," she says, "I thought I would ask my friends if they knew of any Arctic projects. You never know."

"Okay, well, keep looking," I tell her. "We'll find something for you."

For me, finding a charity was a no-brainer. I chose an organization called Polar Bears Forever. I've done lots of research, and I've made information sheets to hand out to the other students. I've even created a PowerPoint slide show with lots of polar-bear pictures.

"Hey, how about this one?" I say to Shanna. "It's called Morning Start. The website talks about the high cost of food up north. This group sends money to schools to make sure the kids start the day with a hot breakfast."

"That sounds good," says Shanna. "What's the web address?" She types it in.

"You're right, my friend," she says. "This Morning Start thing is a good one. I'm going to do my presentation on it. There's tons of info, so it will be easy to pull something together by Monday."

"Will you do a PowerPoint?" I ask. "Or make posters and handouts? I know! You could make a breakfast. You can tell everyone how much it cost you to make it here. Then find out how much the ingredients would cost in the North."

Shanna shuts her computer down.

"Like, find out how much you pay for an egg here and how much you'd have to pay for it in the Arctic!" I say. "Then you can compare costs on a chart."

"Yeah, good idea," she says. "I'll think about that. Let's get outta here."

Chapter Four

Unlike last Saturday, today is a good day on the job. I spend the morning spreading mucky compost all over the gardens at the Finch house. Then I wash every light fixture at Mrs. Low's place. I am up and down a ladder for two hours.

Mrs. Naulty doesn't do anything weird today. I finish sweeping and tidying her garage this afternoon, since I didn't get it done last week. The fire-alarm thing messed up my schedule.

It's a long, dirty day, but I'm happy winter is finally over. March is the beginning of the spring-cleaning and yard-work season—and that means I'll finally start making decent money again. Today is the best day I've had in months!

When I get home, I go straight to my room and dump the contents of my bag onto my bed. I wear this tiny cross-body bag when I'm working. It keeps my money safer than if I just stuffed it into my pockets.

When I empty the bag today, I have three ten-dollar bills from Mr. Finch and a twenty from Mrs. Low.

As usual, there's a flowery pink envelope from Mrs. Naulty.

I fire up the computer to put today's earnings—sixty dollars—into my spreadsheet. While it's booting up, I tear open Mrs. N.'s envelope. Why does she bother putting the money in an envelope every week? It's such a waste. I should start giving them back to her.

I stop cold. Today, the envelope doesn't contain the usual pair of five-dollar bills. This time, there are two *$100* bills in there.

Are you kidding me?? Just when I thought nothing weird was going to happen today.

Mrs. Naulty is totally nuts.

What a big fat hassle. Now I have to go back to her house and tell her she messed up. Again. She's getting so confused. How could she mistake a *100* on a bill for a *5*? The numbers don't look anything alike. What a pain in the butt. *She's* such a pain in the butt.

I stare at the money. I don't get to see $100 bills very often. Grandpa gave me one for my birthday last year.

But otherwise, they are rare in my world. One-hundred-dollar bills look so much more impressive than regular money. And there they are, two of them, sitting on my bed. That's a lot of moolah.

I worked hard today. All I want to do is lie in bed and see if there's anything new on Facebook. I do *not* feel like going back over to Mrs. Naulty's. And I sure do not want to explain yet another screw-up to her.

I'll just end up making tea for her. And a sandwich. Maybe I should just keep her money. That would be easier for everyone.

If I kept her two hundred bucks, Mrs. Naulty wouldn't feel stupid. Roger wouldn't think she's crazy and stuff her in an old folks' home. And I would be that much closer to my SUN goal.

Don't even think about it. I shake my head. *I cannot keep this money.*

But what would it hurt if I add the two hundred bucks to my Excel total? Just to see.

I delete the $60 I added a couple of minutes ago. I put in $250 instead. I hit *Enter*.

I stare at the new total at the bottom of the spreadsheet—$5,225.

That is seriously close to the early-bird price for the SUN trip.

The early-bird deadline is only a week away now. With this extra cash, I'm only $275 short. Mom and Dad would totally lend that to me if it meant I could save $2,000.

Now that it's spring, I'll have more work. I'll be able to pay them back in a few weeks. Otherwise, it's going to take me months to earn the full fee.

I don't know what to do.

It's *possible* that Mrs. Naulty meant to give me two $100 bills this week. Maybe it's a tip for all the work I've done for her. Sometimes my clients give me tips.

She probably realizes that she should have been paying me more all along, and she wants to make up for it. The truth is that she actually *should* be paying me more. For all the time I've put in, she *easily* owes me $200. Probably even more than that. No, Mrs. Naulty messed up. There's no way she meant to pay me *twenty* times what she usually gives me.

"Lindy," Mom calls. "Dinner's ready."

I realize I'm starving. My stomach is even growling. "Coming," I yell.

I'll have to figure out all of this later. I stuff the money back into my bag, lock it in my desk drawer and head to the kitchen.

Chapter Five

Every Sunday morning, I go to the ATM to deposit my Saturday earnings. Today, though, I can't seem to get myself there. I've been circling the neighborhood on my bike for an hour. Riding around and around while crazy thoughts roll around and around in my brain.

I can't decide what to do about Mrs. Naulty's money. I cycle past her house for the third time. Roger's car is still in the driveway. He's been there all morning.

I keep riding. I can't return Mrs. Naulty's money while Roger is there. I don't want to make her look stupid in front of him. If he finds out how much his grandmother has been screwing up lately, he'll send her away for sure.

But I can't keep riding around forever.

I have no choice. I go to the ATM and deposit $250. The deposit envelope feels fatter than usual. It's not. One-hundred-dollar bills aren't any thicker than five-dollar bills. But it feels bigger somehow.

On my way home, I pass Mrs. Naulty's house one last time. Roger's car is gone now, but it's too late. The money's in the bank.

I hate to admit it, but I'm pretty excited. It's as if the universe is telling me that Mrs. Naulty's money is meant for me. Polar bears, here I come.

I burst into the house. Mom and Dad are lounging in the living room. I have my Sunday ritual—going to the ATM. They have theirs—drinking tea and reading the newspaper in their pj's.

I have to be careful what I say to them right now. Mom and Dad think I'm hundreds of dollars short of the SUN trip early-bird fee. But I have an idea. When they ask how I managed to make so much in the past few weeks, I'm going to tell them that I made a mistake on my spreadsheet. "Guess what?" I grin.

"What's up, buttercup?" Dad says. He thinks he's so funny.

"I just deposited the money I earned yesterday," I say. "And..."

"And you have enough to buy us a new car?"

Very funny. I give him the Dad-don't-be-a-goofball look.

"Sorry, kid." He snickers. "What were you going to say?"

"The early-bird deadline is next week, and I almost have enough for the early-bird fee."

"*Almost?*" says Mom. "How close is *almost?*"

"I only need $275 more. And if you could loan that to me, I could pay you back in a few weeks. It's spring now. I'm getting lots of work. So it won't take long at all."

Neither of them asks how I managed to make so much money so quickly.

"So…?" I put on my best puppy-dog face.

"What do you think, Janet?" Dad says. "Can we afford to loan the girl $275?"

"I promise I'll pay you back really soon," I vow. "Cross my heart." I do it to prove I'm serious.

"Well," says Mom slowly, "I suppose we could manage that…"

I shriek. Dad covers his ears. I hug him. "Thank you!" I hug Mom. "This is amazing! You are the best parents ever!"

"Remember that next time we ask you to mow the lawn," Dad says with a laugh.

I sprint to the back door. "I have to tell Asha and Claire," I call as I run outside.

Asha and Claire are my best friends. I've known them my whole life. We all live on the same block, and we walk to school together. We do almost every-thing together.

I get to Asha's house first. It's closer. I knock on her door, and when she answers I grab her hand. "We have to go to Claire's," I tell her. "I have something to tell you both. Together."

"Okay, okay. Can I at least put some shoes on?" Then she yells, "Mom! I'm going to Claire's with Lindy."

I drag her across the street to Claire's house. When we're all together, I blurt it out.

"As of ten minutes ago, it became officially official. I am going to the Arctic this summer!" I'm practically jumping up and down as I tell them all the details.

They shriek and throw their arms around me. They know how badly I want to go on this trip.

"Lindy, we knew you would get there," says Claire. "We knew you would get to see a polar bear one day!"

They also know how hard I've worked to earn the money to pay for this trip.

"That is amazing, Lindy!" says Asha. "You did it!"

I don't tell them about keeping Mrs. Naulty's $200.

Chapter Six

I've barely been able to focus on my classes today. Mondays are always a drag, but today is unbearable. All I want to do is get to the Northern Discovery Club meeting after school. I can't wait to tell everyone that it's official. That Mom paid for my SUN trip online yesterday. That I'm actually going to the Arctic in August!

Everyone will be so excited. And so jealous. They all know I was accepted for the SUN trip. But nobody—including me—knew whether I'd be able to raise enough money in time. It's all so crazy, I can hardly believe it's true.

My last class of the day is English. We're studying *Romeo and Juliet* by William Shakespeare. My teacher, Mr. Plue—or Mr. Pee-yoo, as we sometimes call him—is cool. Today, he's letting us watch a movie version of the play. It's really old. It's from 1996, and it stars Leonardo DiCaprio. It's funny because he's so young.

Normally, I would be happy watching a movie in class. But today, I just want to get out of here. It's too dark to see the clock. And if I pull out my phone to check the time, Mr. Plue will see the light, and I'll get in trouble. So I'm squirming in my chair, trying to figure out how long until the class is over and

I can go to the Northern Discovery Club to share my excellent news.

At last the movie stops, and Mr. Plue turns the lights on. "We'll have to leave it there until next class," he says. "Meanwhile, think about some of the ways this film made *Romeo and Juliet* relevant to modern audiences." Nobody is listening to him. We're all packing up our stuff.

Yeah, yeah. Just let me out of here so I can go see Ms. Komiuk. She is going to flip when she hears my news.

Ms. Komiuk teaches geography, and she is in charge of the Northern Discovery Club. She's Inuit. She grew up in the Northwest Territories, in a village called Tuktoyaktuk. We have learned so much from her in the last six months.

We're not supposed to run in the hallways, so I walk as fast as I can. I'm sure I look like one of those dorky speed walkers with my bum hitching side to side. I don't even stop at my locker to ditch my books. I want to get to Ms. Komiuk's room before anyone else arrives. I want her to be the first to know.

I can barely breathe by the time I get to room 207. She's alone.

"Ms. Komiuk," I wheeze as I burst in on her, "I have something to tell you!"

"Lindy, what's wrong?" She looks worried.

"No, it's something good. It's actually something *amazing*!"

I spit out my big news. She is so excited that she throws her arms around me. "Lindy, this is wonderful. Congratulations! I am so proud of you for making this happen!"

We laugh and speak in exclamation marks for the next five minutes.

Eventually, other students start filing into the classroom.

"What's going on?" asks Shanna.

"Lindy has an announcement, but let's wait until everyone is here," Ms. Komiuk says, smiling.

The Northern Discovery Club only has eight members, but it takes forever for all of them to arrive today. As usual, Austin is the last into the room. We're always waiting for him. Finally, he dashes in and takes a place in the circle.

"Our first order of business today is an exciting announcement," says Ms. Komiuk. She nods to me. "Go ahead, Lindy."

I can't stop smiling as I announce my good news. Everyone claps and cheers. They seem truly thrilled for me.

"Have you met any of the other students yet?" asks Paige.

"I wonder how cold it is in summer," says James. "Do they supply all the food and clothes and stuff?"

"What do you have to do next?" Alex wants to know.

Wow. So many questions. They're all talking at once. I can't get a word in!

"How'd you pay for it so soon?" Shanna's voice booms out over all the others.

She knows I was hundreds of dollars short of the early-bird deadline. I don't know what to say.

Thankfully, Austin butts in. "You'll have to get a kick-ass camera," he says. "One that takes excellent video too. We want to see polar bears, Lindy."

"You'll have to post pictures every single day," agrees Paige.

The questions keep coming. I make sure *not* to look at Shanna. If she asks me about money again, I'll tell her what I was going to tell Mom and Dad—that I made a mistake on my spreadsheet.

Ms. Komiuk saves me. "We're all excited about Lindy's trip," she says. "And I'm sure she will share more information over the coming months.

Right now, though, let's get our meeting back on track."

For the next ninety minutes, we all make presentations about the Arctic charities we want to support. Today's goal is to narrow our eight choices down to two. We're not allowed to vote for our own organization. That means I have to do a brilliant presentation so everyone else will vote for Polar Bears Forever.

Some of the presentations are lame. Shanna's is the worst. I gave her all kinds of ideas, but all she does is read from the Morning Start website.

Austin makes a serious presentation about teen suicide in remote Arctic villages. He tells us that the suicide rate among Inuit youth is eleven times higher than in the rest of Canada. The program he wants us to support is called Project Northern Life. It trains Inuit youth to recognize the warning signs of suicide, and teaches them how to help each other survive.

When it comes time to vote, I choose Austin's charity.

Before the end of the meeting, Ms. Komiuk counts the votes. "The two finalists are...drum roll please... Project Northern Life and Polar Bears Forever." We all clap. "Your homework is to research both charities. Next month, we will discuss the merits of the two organizations and choose the one that the Northern Discovery Club will support."

I'm excited that my polar-bear charity could be the winner. But I'm even more excited about my SUN trip. "Shanna, wait up," I call to my friend. "Let's walk home together."

Chapter Seven

On the way home, I can't help myself. I babble on about my SUN trip. "Just think! Five months from now, I'll be in the Arctic!" I gush.

Shanna doesn't say anything.

"I'll have to make a list of everything I need to get for the trip. Austin is right. First thing I need is a good camera. And good boots. Waterproof.

Maybe a new jacket. Mine probably won't be warm enough."

Shanna seems deep in thought. I'm not sure she's listening to me. But nothing can crush my SUN spirit right now. I'm practically skipping down the street!

"I mean, it will be summer, so it could be up to thirty degrees Celsius on land. But when we're out on the water, it will be freezing cold. And crazy windy. It's totally unpredictable. At least the wind will keep the swarms of mosquitoes away. Still, I should get a bug jacket and—"

"How did you meet the early-bird deadline?" Shanna butts in. "Last I heard, you were something like eight hundred bucks short."

Way to shut me down. "I made a mistake on my spreadsheet," I say. "And I saved $2,000 by paying this week. So I didn't need as much money, and…well, I made a mistake."

"A mistake? Seriously? You're obsessed with that spreadsheet and all your calculations. You count every nickel and dime. No way you—"

"Hey, let's go in here," I say. We're in front of Jazzy's convenience store. I pass it every day on the way home. Normally I don't go in, but I want to shut Shanna up about the SUN money. "I have a craving for Twizzlers."

The little bell dingles as I push open the door. A few other kids are already there, checking out the candy counter. Jazzy's is kind of a neighborhood hangout.

I'm hoping to distract Shanna from the whole SUN thing.

"Go ask the doofus at the till when they're going to get the next issue of *Canadian Geographic* magazine," Shanna says quietly. "The shelf is empty."

"Since when do you read *Canadian Geographic*?"

"Just go." Shanna gives me a little shove.

"Okay, okay." I head to the counter. Shanna is so weird sometimes.

I don't know this particular clerk. I've seen him once or twice before, but he's new to the shop. His name tag says *Ben*. He is kind of cute and not much older than I am.

"Hi," I say when the customer ahead of me is done. "I have a question about *Canadian Geographic* magazine. The shelf is empty. Do you know when the next issue will be in the store?"

"Ummm, I'm not sure," he says. "Just a sec. I'll look it up for you."

He crouches down and digs under the counter, rustling papers and notebooks around. Eventually, he stands up with a binder in his hands. "*Canadian Geographic. Canadian Geographic. Canadian Geographic.*" His finger traces a list of magazine names.

"Okay. Here it is. That magazine comes out every two months. Next issue is the April edition, which will be in the store…" He's reading while he's talking. "It looks like it should be here in about two weeks."

By this time, Shanna has joined me at the counter.

"Okay, thanks for checking," I say to Ben. Then I turn to Shanna. "He says it will be here in a couple of weeks. Is there an article you want to read?"

"Yeah, I heard there's going to be something about polar bears in it."

"Really?" My eyes light up. She grabs my arm.

"Yup. C'mon. I have to get going." She thanks the clerk sweetly as she pulls me toward the door.

"Bye." I wave to Ben as we make our way to the door. "How do you know there's going to be a story about polar bears?" I ask Shanna. "I can't wait to read it. I'll have to get a copy of the magazine too. I'll have to tell Ms. Komiuk."

Shanna doesn't say anything. But once we're outside, she bursts out laughing. "There's no polar bear article, you loser! I had to tell the counter jockey something to get you out of there."

I'm confused.

Until we're about half a block away. Then she pulls a giant package of Twizzlers out from under her coat.

"What…"

"You said you wanted Twizzlers, my friend. So I got you some Twizzlers." She rips open the bag and holds it out to me.

I don't know what to do. She just stole candy. For me. It's wrong, but kind of sweet at the same time.

"Well? Aren't you going to take some? I thought you wanted Twizzlers." She actually looks hurt that I'm not oozing with gratitude.

"Well, yeah. But I didn't mean for you to steal them."

"Seriously? I'm pretty sure neither of us has any money. How did you think we were going to get them?"

She pauses and pulls two sticks of red licorice out of the bag. She hands me one. I don't take it.

"Wait a minute." She waves a Twizzler at me. "Don't tell me you've never stolen anything before."

I don't know what to say. If I say no, she'll think I'm a complete dork. If I say yes, well, I'd be lying. Sort of.

"Ha! I should have known." Shanna shakes her head and rolls her eyes. "Of course. You are a total Goody-Two-Shoes."

She starts walking away from me. She's right—I *am* a loser.

"I have too," I blurt out before I can stop myself. I run to catch up with her. I grab a stick of licorice from her hand.

"I have too stolen before. And I've stolen *way* more than a measly bag of Twizzlers."

She stops and stares at me. Ha! She doesn't know what to say now that she realizes I'm cool after all.

"You? *You* have stolen something? Like what?"

"Like money—and *lots* of it," I say casually. I start strolling down the sidewalk, forcing *her* to catch up with *me* now.

"How much?" Shanna asks.

"A *lot*," I say.

"What, like twenty-five cents?" She doesn't believe me.

"Nope. More like…" I pause for effect. "More like *two hundred bucks*," says the cool kid I've suddenly become.

"When did this happen?"

"On the weekend." I lower my voice. "I took it from Mrs. Naulty's house when I worked for her on Saturday."

"I *knew* it!" Shanna cries. "*That's* how you paid for your trip. I knew there was no way you'd earned enough on your own. And I knew for *sure* that you hadn't made a mistake on your spreadsheet."

We reach the corner where we go our separate ways. Shanna high-fives me before she turns the corner. "Nicely done, sister!"

Chapter Eight

"Earth to Lindy."

"Huh?"

"Let me guess," says Asha. "You're thinking about your trip again."

Claire chimes in, "Lindy, I know this is hard for you to believe, but there are *actually* other things going on in the world." She laughs. Claire is always laughing.

Tuesday is my favorite day of the week. It's the one day I get to have lunch with these two. But today I'm not really enjoying our cafeteria time.

I can't stop thinking about my walk home last night with Shanna. I'm wondering if I should have told her about Mrs. Naulty's money. Saying it to Shanna somehow made it more real. Before I said it out loud, it was as if it wasn't real money and Mrs. Naulty wasn't a real person. When I was bragging about it last night, I felt like a take-charge sort of girl who goes after what she wants. Why do I feel all weird about it today?

I certainly can't talk to Claire and Asha about any of this. They've known Mrs. Naulty forever too. I can't let them know that I kept her money. They would never forgive me.

"I asked you about the math test," says Asha. "How do you think you did?"

She stuffs a huge bite of her tuna sandwich into her mouth.

"Oh, okay, I think."

Asha is still chewing, so I keep talking. "It didn't really feel like a test to me. Algebra is all about solving puzzles. It's a challenge, but I like figuring it out."

"I'm pretty sure I bombed the test," sighs Claire. She takes a sip of lemonade. "Oh no. There's your Northern Discovery Club friend. I hope you two aren't going to go all Arctic on us." She rolls her eyes in a fake sort of way.

I look over my shoulder to see Shanna scanning the cafeteria. When she sees me, she makes a beeline for our table.

"Hi, Shanna," chirps Claire. She's the friendliest person I've ever known. I love that about her.

"Yeah. Hi." Shanna is not the friendliest person I've ever known.

Shanna leans over and whispers in my ear. "I need to talk to you."

"Sure. What?" I say.

"In private," says Shanna.

"Can I at least finish my lunch first?" I say.

"No. It's important. Come now." Shanna sounds so serious that my stomach does a little flip.

She drags me across the cafeteria and outside into the March chill. "Geez, Shanna. I don't even have a coat on. Do we really have to talk outside? What's the big secret?"

"Oh suck it up, sister."

Wow. Somebody's in a foul mood.

"Listen," she says. "Does anyone else know about the $200 you got from the old lady?"

I shake my head. "Nope."

"Not even your lunch buddies?"

"No. Why?"

"Well, I've been thinking about it since you told me yesterday…"

I cut her off. "I don't want to talk about it anymore."

I know what's coming. Shanna is about to lecture me about how I should not have kept Mrs. Naulty's money

Like I haven't been thinking about that enough.

"It's freezing out here. I'm going in."

Shanna grabs my arm as I turn toward the building. Just like she did in Jazzy's convenience store yesterday. *Now what?*

"Like I said," she says. "I've been thinking about that two hundred bucks all night."

"Yeah. And?"

"And I want a cut."

I laugh out loud. "What are you, the mob or something?" I pull my arm away.

"I think you can afford to share some of that money you make on Saturdays with your new BFF Shanna."

"Are you out of your mind?" I stop laughing.

Shanna is scary serious right now.

"Here's how our partnership is going to work," she says as if I haven't spoken. "You're going to keep your sweet little Saturday business up and running. And every Monday, you're going to give me half of your earnings."

She smiles, so I laugh again. She is totally messing with me!

But her smile is not a real smile. It's a creepy, ugly grin.

I shiver. And it's not because of the cold air.

"Why would I do that?" I ask carefully.

"Because if you don't, I'm going to spill your big secret."

Now Shanna laughs. "It will be so sad when you lose your scholarship for the SUN program. In fact, I bet you won't even get to go on the trip at all."

What is she saying?

"I'm pretty sure the SUN people don't consider ripping off little old ladies to be role-model behavior. Some people might even call it elder abuse. That's a low thing to do, Little Miss Businesswoman."

I feel sick. Shanna is right. Those are the rules. If my grades drop or I stop being a good role model, I will be kicked off the SUN trip.

"You know it wasn't like that, Shanna," I whisper. "I don't rip off little old ladies. It was a mistake. Plus, for your information, I've been doing a lot of thinking since yesterday too."

Shanna shrugs her shoulders.

"I've decided to work for Mrs. Naulty for free until I pay back all her money. No harm, no foul."

"It's a bit late for that, partner. The deed is done."

Her nasty confidence kills me.

"No, my friend, I think you will keep up your Saturday schedule, and you will give me half of your take. Or I spill the beans."

"I thought you were my friend," I say.

"Because I joined your stupid polar bear club?" she scoffs. "Seriously? I *had* to join extracurricular activities. This is the only school I've ever heard of where hobbies are mandatory."

How did I not see how mean this girl is?

"Nope," Shanna continues. "I only hang out with you so you'll do my assignments. And I picked the club that you northern bright-lights are in because it is the only one that meets only once a month. The rest meet too often for my schedule. Plus, I kinda like polar bears and penguins. They're cute."

I can't believe what I'm hearing.

"Penguins live in the Antarctic, you idiot," I say coldly. "Haven't you learned anything in the past six months?" I want her to feel as dumb as I feel for having trusted her.

"Oh, I've learned all I need to know," Shanna sneers. "Brrrrrrr. It's a bit chilly out here, don't you think? I'm going in. See you next Monday. Bring your wallet."

She turns and strides toward the cafeteria door.

This can't be happening.

Chapter Nine

I stand outside in the cold for so long that Asha and Claire come looking for me. They yell to me from the cafeteria door.

"Lindy, what are you doing?" Asha's voice jolts me back to reality. "Come on. We're going to be late for class."

I join them, shivering as I enter the warm lunchroom.

"What was so important that Shanna had to drag you outside?" asks Claire. We quickly gather our stuff and start walking toward our next classes.

I can't tell my friends the truth about my conversation with Shanna. If I do, I'll also have to tell them I stole from Mrs. Naulty.

"Shanna has math class now." I'm surprised at how easily I come up with a fib. "She knows we just took the test. She wanted me to give her the answers."

So now I'm a thief and a liar.

"I knew there was something about her I didn't like," says Asha. "I hope you didn't help her cheat."

"Of course not," I reply—as if I'm the most honorable person in the world.

We split up in the hallway. Asha and Claire have history next. I head to French class.

I spend the rest of the day in a daze, kicking myself for being so stupid, for trusting someone I barely know. All this time, I've been working with Shanna on club projects, being nice to her, being a *friend*.

And now she's *blackmailing* me!

Thankfully, I don't see her for the rest of the week.

In fact, other than Shanna's creepiness that one day, it's a totally normal week at school and at home. I hang out with Claire and Asha like always. I message back and forth with the SUN kids on our private Facebook page. I write an essay for French class about which animal I would like to be if I could be one. Regular stuff.

By the weekend, my chilly Tuesday chat with Shanna has pretty much faded from my brain. I'm convinced that I must have misunderstood what she was talking about. No way she would demand money from me like that. That only happens in the movies.

On Saturday, I work for Mrs. Naulty as usual. And she gives me two five-dollar bills in a flowery pink envelope.

This time, though, I don't keep her money. Before I leave her house, I take the cash out of the envelope and stash it in a kitchen drawer. Mrs. Naulty will find it and assume she put it there herself.

It will take me forever to pay her back like this. But it's the only way I can think of to do it. I don't want her to feel bad for screwing up, and I don't want to give Roger any more reasons to send his grandma away.

I also help Mr. Finch on Saturday. He has more dirty garden chores for me. And I run a few errands for a new client, a lady who heard about me from Mr. Finch.

As soon as I get home from work, I find Mom and Dad. I hand them a twenty-dollar bill, the first installment in the $275 I owe them.

They've decided that they don't want me to give them *all* of my earnings. They only want twenty dollars a week. That way, they say, I'll always have money in my pocket. And I'll still be able to pay them back long before I go to the Arctic.

On Sunday morning, I don't bother going to the ATM. Now that I've paid my SUN fees, I can actually keep a little money for myself.

It's a killer spring day, so I text Claire and Asha to ask if they want to go for a bike ride. Asha is busy with her family, but Claire is up for it.

We ride around the neighborhood, eventually ending up at Jazzy's convenience store. I hope cute-new-cashier Ben is there today.

"Let's get Twizzlers," I say to Claire as we park our bikes. "My treat!"

It turns out that cute-new-cashier Ben *is* on duty at Jazzy's today.

"Hey, you're the *Canadian Geographic* girl," he says when we walk in. I'm flattered he remembers.

"I'm Ben."

"I know," I say, pointing to his name tag. "I'm Lindy. She's Claire."

"Nice to meet you, Lindy and Claire," he says with a smile.

I'm suddenly too shy to speak. I grab Claire and head to the Twizzlers.

"He's cute," Claire whispers. "I can see why you wanted to come to Jazzy's today."

"Shhh," I tell her, glancing over my shoulder at Ben. He's helping a customer at the counter.

The customer is still there when we go to pay. I dig out my money while I'm waiting for my turn at the till. I'm hoping that buying a package of Twizzlers today will make up for the one Shanna stole for me last week.

Ben bags the man's bread, milk and peanut butter, then picks up my package of red licorice. He scans it. I hand him my money without looking at him. "So I guess I'll see you next week," he says.

"Uhhh," is the brilliant reply I come up with before I turn to leave. I'm sure my face is as red as the candy I just bought.

"The new issue of *Canadian Geographic* will be here by then. I'll save you a copy."

"Umm…Okay…Thanks…Bye," is all I can spit out.

"I'm here every Sunday," Ben calls as Claire and I head for the door.

Claire barely makes it outside before she starts batting her eyelashes and making kissy noises at me. "*Okay, Ben. Thanks, Ben. Bye, Ben.*"

"Oh, you are so hilarious." I roll my eyes and gave her a little swat. We giggle all the way home.

Chapter Ten

Of course, this morning on the way to school, Claire has to tell Asha every detail of yesterday's visit to Jazzy's. They tease me. But I know they're as pumped as I am that a cute boy maybe likes me. This week is off to a good start!

Still, I feel a little twinge of anxiety at school this morning. I keep my eyes peeled for Shanna. Just in case.

I'm especially edgy at lunchtime, since that's when she nabbed me last Tuesday.

But the day comes and goes with no sign of her. And no demands for money.

I *knew* it! I knew she was just messing with me last week. There's no way she'd actually blackmail me.

After my last class of the day, I go to my locker. I organize my books and pack my knapsack with homework. I pull out my coat, put it on and slam the locker shut.

Then I practically jump out of my skin. Shanna is suddenly right in front of me. Geez, she's sneaky. Totally freaks me out.

"I believe you owe me some money," she says sweetly.

"Shanna, back off. I'm not giving you anything. This isn't funny."

"I agree. It isn't funny."

We stare at each other for a moment.

"Shanna, listen." I try to reason with her. "This doesn't make any sense. If you need money, maybe we can talk to—"

"The only person I'm talking to is you, Arctic Annie. We have an arrangement. You cough up the cash, or I report a theft—to the tune of $200."

I don't know what to do. I can't pay her. But I can't *not* pay her.

Shanna sighs and shrugs. "Okay, room 207, Ms. Komiuk, here I come."

She turns and marches down the hall. Toward Ms. Komiuk's room.

"Wait," I cry. "You win."

I only made forty dollars this weekend because of not keeping Mrs. Naulty's ten. I feel like throwing up as I riffle through my bag.

Shanna saunters back to my locker. I hand her a twenty.

"Not your best week. But thank you, Lindy. So generous of you."

What have I gotten myself into?

The following Monday, I try to outwit Shanna. I make sure I'm not alone all day long. I make sure Claire or Asha or a teacher…or *somebody*… is with me at all times. And it works! Shanna is nowhere to be seen.

The next day, though, I let my guard down. And the second I'm alone, she slithers up to me with her hand out.

"Nice try," she says. "You can't hide from me, Lindy. If I don't get my money on Monday, I'll get it on Tuesday. Or Wednesday. Doesn't matter to me."

What a creep.

"Now, hand it over," she orders. I don't have the energy to run away or continue hiding from her. I give her twenty-five dollars.

Another week passes, and another Monday rolls around. All day I'm a nervous wreck waiting for Shanna to pop up and demand money. But I have a new strategy today. I've thought of a way to *not* give Shanna any money this week.

When she sneaks up to me at my locker after lunch, I'm ready.

"Oh, hi, Shanna," I say coolly. I'm pleased with myself and my plan. "Sorry, but I have nothing for you this week. I took the weekend off."

"You didn't work?" She sounds surprised.

"Nope."

"Not at all?"

"No. So get lost."

Shanna doesn't move. *Ha! She doesn't know what to do now that I've outsmarted her!*

"That's funny," she purrs. "I could have sworn I saw you go into old lady Low's house on Saturday. What were you doing there if you weren't working? Having a tea party?"

My stomach sinks.

"And you mean that wasn't you I saw planting flower bulbs with the old geezer in the red brick house?"

I was in Mr. Finch's backyard. No way she could have seen me there. Unless…

"It's not nice to lie to your business partner, Lindy."

"And it's totally psycho to spy on people, Shanna."

"I don't *spy*, Snowflake. I protect my business interests. So give me thirty bucks, and I'll pretend you didn't try to weasel out of our agreement this week."

"This is nuts. *You* are nuts."

"Do not mess with me, Lindy. Unless you want to kiss your Arctic adventure goodbye."

I don't know what to do other than dig through my bag to find some cash for her.

Shanna pockets my money and strolls away. "See you next week, partner!"

I lean against my locker, on the verge of tears.

Three weeks ago, I was bursting with excitement about my SUN trip. Now, I may not even get to go because of Shanna. She has ruined everything.

Chapter Eleven

I'm a basket case because of Shanna's blackmail scheme.

On the way to school Wednesday, I almost wet myself when a passing car backfires. "Lindy, what is up with you?" Asha asks. "You're so jumpy lately."

"My mom and I had a big fight this morning," I say. I'm getting good at lying.

I can't tell Claire and Asha the truth. They would hate me for what I did to Mrs. Naulty.

At school, I can barely focus. I even get a C on a math test. I never get anything below an A in that class. The teacher is so concerned that she makes me stay late. To *talk* about it.

So I make up another story—this time about not studying for the test because my cat died. I've never had a cat. But Ms. Gaertner buys it. Even hugs me.

"Oh, Lindy, I'm so sorry. I know how hard it is to say goodbye to our furry friends."

I bite my lip, stare at the floor and look as sad as I can until she lets me leave.

At home I barely leave my bedroom these days. Mom and Dad think I have more homework than usual or I'm on Facebook with my SUN friends. They pretty much leave me alone.

The truth is, the only thing I do these days is try to figure out how to get Shanna off my back. It's all I think about.

If I don't pay Shanna half my earnings, she will tell Ms. Komiuk that I stole from an old lady—and I will be kicked off the SUN trip.

But if I keep paying her…Well, what then?

When will it end? How will it ever stop? Even if I only pay Shanna until after the SUN trip, that's still more than four months of this.

My brain runs in circles. I can't shut it off. And I can't come up with a way to shut Shanna down.

The only way to stop paying her is to stop working on Saturdays. For real.

But then who would help Mr. Finch and Mrs. Naulty and the others?

Today was my best Saturday on the job so far this year. I made seventy bucks. Or, I should say, thirty-five because… well, because of Shanna's share.

As I always do now before I leave Mrs. Naulty's house, I stash her pair of five-dollar bills in a kitchen drawer for her to find later.

If I could snap my fingers and turn back time, I would give Mrs. Naulty back her $200. Right away. Like I should have done in the first place.

Everything is so messed up. And it's killing me.

My brain is going around in circles as I ride home. It's still driving me crazy when I park my bike in the backyard and go into the house. All I want to do is lie down on my bed and forget about Shanna. And Mrs. Naulty. And the money. Even the SUN trip.

No such luck.

"Lindy, come in here, please," Mom calls from the living room. "Before you go to your room. I need to talk to you about something."

This can't be good. Instantly, panic rises into my throat. She must have found out about Mrs. Naulty's money. What am I going to do? What am I going to say?

I take off my coat and boots as slowly as I can. I hang them up carefully. I stop in the kitchen for a glass of orange juice. I need time to think, to come up with an explanation before I face Mom.

"Lindy, are you all right?" She looks alarmed. "You're as white as a sheet."

"I'm fine. Just a bit tired."

Mom stares at me with a weird look on her face.

"What?" I snip. "What's so urgent?"

"I need to know what's going on with Mrs. Naulty."

"What are you talking about?"

"What I'm talking about, Lin, is Mrs. Naulty and how she's doing. Is everything okay with her?"

"Of course. Sure. Why wouldn't it be?" I'm not going to give her any hints. If she wants to know about the money, she'll have to ask.

"Well, a few weeks ago, you were worried about her. You said she'd been doing strange things."

I breathe a huge sigh of relief. In all the Shanna drama, I totally forgot that I'd told Mom about Mrs. Naulty losing her marbles. Or getting dementia, I should say.

"Oh, that. Nope, nothing since then. Nothing unusual at all." *For example, she never gave me twenty times my pay one day. Nope.*

"I phoned Roger after you told me about the toaster oven," Mom says.

"He's been visiting her more often since then to keep an eye on her."

I feel like I've ratted out my grandma.

"She's definitely getting forgetful. And it's getting worse all the time." Mom takes a deep breath before continuing. "Lindy, Roger phoned me while you were out today. He has started looking into other options for his grandmother."

"What does that mean, *other options*?" I ask the question, but I already know the answer.

"Lindy, there are some lovely retirement homes in town."

"No!"

"If Mrs. Naulty moves to a home, she won't be alone anymore," Mom says. "We won't have to worry about her burning down the house or letting con men into her kitchen."

"But it would be like jail," I cry.

"Not at all," Mom says softly. "These places are designed for independent living. Mrs. Naulty would have her own apartment. She could come and go as she pleases. She would have her meals in a nice dining room. And there would be outings and activities and clubs she could join."

She's going to be sent away, and it's all my fault! I should have kept my big mouth shut.

I can't help it. The tears start falling.

"I don't want her to go to an old-folks' home," I sob. "If I hadn't told you those things about her, Roger wouldn't think she's going crazy. And he wouldn't be sending her away. She could stay home."

Mom rushes to my side and puts her arm around me. "Lindy, the most important thing is that Mrs. Naulty is safe. And she may not be safe at home anymore."

No matter what Mom says, I can't stop bawling.

I don't want Mrs. Naulty to leave. I don't want it to be because of me.

"Lindy, it will be okay," Mom says, trying to soothe me.

No, it won't, I scream inside my head. *Mrs. Naulty is going away because of me. And I took $200 from her. And I'm being blackmailed. And I don't know what to do about any of it. My whole life is falling apart!*

Out loud, I manage to choke out a few words between sobs. "I just can't imagine Mrs. Naulty not being here anymore, Mom. She's always been there for me."

And look at how I've repaid her...

Chapter Twelve

I've started to hate Mondays. Mondays mean Shanna is going to crawl out from under her rock and come after me for cash. Sometime during the day, somewhere in the school, she'll sneak up on me when no one else is around. I don't even bother trying to hide from her anymore.

Today, though, I am not in the mood for her psycho self. I can't do this anymore. It has to stop. I have to *make* her stop.

At the end of the day, as I'm packing my homework into my knapsack, Shanna slinks up to my locker.

"Howdy, pardner," she drawls. "How much moolah did we earn this week?"

"We? Shanna, there is no *we*." I've had it with her. "*I* work. *I* earn money. *You* do nothing. And today, you *get* nothing." I slam the locker door shut, an audio exclamation mark.

"I am so done with you!" I yell. "You're a lunatic and a loser. And a total bully. I am not giving you another nickel. No wonder you have no friends. What is wrong with you?"

Shanna actually looks a little hurt. "Oh my gosh. Maybe you're right," she pouts. "Maybe I *am* being mean. Maybe I *should* stop asking you for money. I should probably leave you alone from now on."

She pauses. Then she bursts out laughing. "As if. Listen, Miss Brain Freeze, if you want to go on your trip, you're going to keep paying for the privilege."

For a second, I thought I'd gotten through to her.

"Or maybe you don't care about seeing polar bears this summer after all. I'll bet Ms. Eskimo Pie would be very interested to hear about how you paid for your trip. How you ripped off a sweet little old lady."

"Don't call her that. Eskimo is a bad word. Ms. Komiuk is Inuit."

"Oh, sorry, didn't mean to insult your Arctic idol," sneers Shanna. "I bet you two rub noses together after club meetings."

"Stop it," I roar. Her racism makes me sick.

I cannot beat this girl. There is no way out.

In frustration, I grab cash out of my bag and throw it at Shanna. "Here. Now leave me alone. Leave Ms. Komiuk out of this. Just…go…"

"You know, Lindy, I don't like your attitude. I think the price of my silence has just gone up. I want another ten dollars for my trouble this week."

I go cold. "What? No."

"Okay then. Have it your way. Off I go to see your Northern Nellie teacher friend."

I stare at her. My mouth is open, but no words come out.

Shanna is oozing cruel confidence, as if she's just won the Hunger Games by shooting an arrow through my heart.

I cannot let her tell Ms. Komiuk about Mrs. Naulty's money.

"I only have five dollars left," I croak. "I gave the rest to my parents."

"Well, let's consider that a down payment," says Shanna. "Next week you can give me half of your take, plus the other five dollars you owe me from today. Plus an extra ten in interest. That's only fair."

She snaps the five-dollar bill out of my hand.

"You really should manage your money better, Penguin."

She turns with a smirk and marches down the hallway.

I stand there with my mouth open. Watching her walk away with my money. Watching her get away with this.

Suddenly, it is crystal clear what I have to do. I hate the idea. But I know it is the only way to get Shanna off my back once and for all.

Chapter Thirteen

I know that what I'm about to do will get me kicked off the Students Up North trip. And Ms. Komiuk will probably hate me forever. But I got myself into this. And only I can get me out of it.

I stand outside room 207 for a long time, psyching myself up. Through the window, I see her marking papers at her desk. I take a deep breath and push open the door.

"Excuse me, Ms. Komiuk." My voice comes out in a squeak.

"Oh, hello, Lindy. We don't have a Northern Discovery Club meeting today. It's next Monday."

"I know. But I want to ask you something. I mean, I need to tell you something. I mean…ummm…do you have a minute?"

My mouth is dry, and I feel like throwing up. But I have to do this. Ms. Komiuk has to hear this from *me*. Not from Shanna. *I* have to be the one to tell her what I did.

I enter the room and close the door behind me. Ms. Komiuk watches me approach the desk. I stand in front of her. Head up, back straight. I feel like I'm about to face a firing squad. I clear my throat.

"Ms. Komiuk," I begin, "I did something that wasn't quite the right thing to do. I was so desperate to go on the SUN trip to the Arctic—and to see a polar bear—that I did something stupid."

Then I confess everything to her.

I tell her how I kept money from Mrs. Naulty that probably wasn't meant for me. "And now I'm lying to everyone so they don't find out. But one person did find out. Well, I accidentally told her."

I tell her how Shanna is now making me give her half of all the money I earn.

"If I don't give her money every week, she says she'll tell you how I stole Mrs. Naulty's money. But I thought if I told you myself, she would have to leave me alone. She can't blackmail me if it's not a secret anymore."

Ms. Komiuk doesn't say a thing as I blurt it all out. She concentrates on every word with a frown on her face. I hate how much I am disappointing her.

"I know I'm no longer a model student," I whisper. "And I know I will be disqualified from the SUN trip now."

But I can't do this anymore. Not only the blackmailing. Everything. The lying, my guilty conscience, my falling grades.

"I need to fix the mess I've made," I tell her.

When I finish blabbing, Ms. Komiuk doesn't move or speak.

By this time, I'm bawling like a baby. I'm crying because I'm ashamed of myself for stealing from an elderly lady who has been nothing but kind to me. I'm crying because I feel like a jerk for lying to my parents, my friends and my favorite teacher. I'm crying because I'm afraid of what's going to happen next.

Weirdly, though, the tears make me feel better. Saying all of this out loud—even if it means I'm going to be punished—means that I'm not in it alone anymore.

Say something, I want to scream at her. *Please, say something!*

I stare at my hands. I watch tears drip onto my fingers, then slide to the floor. I wish I could dissolve into that puddle of shame with them.

After what feels like hours, Ms. Komiuk finally makes a move. She takes a sip from the cup of tea on her desk. She holds the mug in both hands. Not speaking, just thinking. Staring into her cup.

At last she looks up and takes a deep breath.

"Okay, Lindy, let's get this sorted out."

She hands me a tissue. Ms. Komiuk is so kind. And I'm such a loser for letting her down.

"First of all, I appreciate that you have come to me," she says. "You did the right thing by letting an adult know what's going on."

I dry my eyes and wipe my nose. She hands me another tissue.

"But this is very serious, Lindy. And there will be consequences."

I nod. I know. I choke back another sob.

Believe me, if I could turn back the clock and have a do-over, I would never…

"What happens next is up to you," she continues. "I can help you figure it out, but you are the only one who can make things right."

I force myself to look at her. "I already know what I have to do, Ms. Komiuk."

Deep breath.

"I have to tell my parents what I did." They are going to kill me.

"Then I have to talk to Mrs. Naulty."

She nods and takes another sip of her tea. I blow my nose again.

"That's a good start," she says. "The sooner you do those things, the better. And you know I'll have to have a talk with your parents, don't you?"

I nod and look at my feet again. I also know she has to report me to the SUN people.

"Is there anything else you want to talk about right now, Lindy?"

Yes. There is one more thing. A really important thing!

But I can't bring myself to ask her what this means for my SUN trip.

"No, Ms. Komiuk."

Chapter Fourteen

I walk home from school by myself, because by the time I leave Ms. Komiuk's room, Claire and Asha are long gone. But it gives me time to come up with a plan for how I will tell my parents what's been going on.

I even practice a few times as I'm walking. I'm sure I look like a crazy person, walking down the street, talking to myself.

By the time Mom and Dad get home from work around five o'clock, I'm ready. I know what I'm going to say.

I wait for them to put away their work stuff. Then they change into comfy clothes. Dad pours two glasses of wine. They check their emails. Which takes forever today.

When they start bustling around the kitchen, I butt in. I can't wait any longer.

"I need to talk to you about something," I blurt out. "Can I talk to you before you get dinner started?"

"What is it, Lin?" Mom gets this panicked look on her face.

"It's just that…I need both of you to listen to me for a minute."

Even Dad looks worried now.

We sit at the kitchen table.

Nobody speaks for a few seconds. I'm too nervous, and they're too freaked out.

"What's up, kid?" Dad tries to sound cool.

Before I lose my nerve, I deliver the speech I've rehearsed. About how I wanted to go on the SUN trip so badly that I made a bad decision. About Shanna. About how I've been lying to everyone.

"I am so sorry," I cry.

Mom has tears in her eyes. Dad looks furious.

Before they can say anything, I continue: "I have a plan though. I know how to fix this."

I have it all figured out!

"If you can loan me another $200, I'll pay Mrs. Naulty back right away," I say. "Then, when school's out for the summer, I'll get another job so I can pay you back even faster. Since I won't be going on the SUN trip now, I'll have lots of time."

That came out poutier than I meant it to.

"I know I have to tell Mrs. Naulty," I add quickly. "I'll do that this weekend. When I go to work for her on Saturday."

Dad is shaking his head. I'm sure he's about to blow up at me.

"Lindy," he says carefully. "Who is Shanna?"

Weird that that's the first thing he asks. But I tell him everything I know about her. Which isn't all that much, I realize. The one thing I don't tell him is that she stole Twizzlers for me. I don't want to have to go to Jazzy's and tell the owner—or Ben—about that.

"Okay, time for supper," Mom says suddenly. She jumps up, goes to the fridge and starts pulling food out. "Rick, why don't you make a salad," she says to Dad.

They make dinner. I set the table. And we keep talking. It's easier to talk when we're not sitting and staring at each other across the table.

We talk about things like temptation and trust. And choosing our friends wisely. And respecting our elders. And fixing our mistakes. All kinds of things I didn't expect to talk about.

By the time dinner is ready, there's only one thing we haven't talked about—my punishment.

"Your father and I need to give that some thought," says Mom. "Meanwhile, you are going to march over to Mrs. Naulty's house tonight. Right after supper. You are going to tell her what you did."

I'm not ready for that yet.

"But Mom, I want to do that on the weekend," I whine.

"No, Lindy. Tonight. This can't wait."

None of us speak much during dinner. We're all deep in thought. I'm working out what to say to Mrs. Naulty.

Mom and Dad are no doubt working out what my punishment will be.

As soon as the table is cleared, Dad practically shoves me out the door.

I trudge down the front steps and along the path. As soon as I reach the sidewalk, I can see Mrs. Naulty's driveway. I can also see Roger's car in the driveway. This is going to be worse than I thought.

Chapter Fifteen

I force myself to ring Mrs. Naulty's doorbell. I'd rather be home in bed, under the covers. Or anywhere else on the planet.

Roger answers the door. A big smile comes to his face when he sees me.

"Lindy! What a surprise. Grandma didn't tell me you were going to be coming over tonight."

"It's a surprise for her too," I chirp, trying to sound at least a little bit happy to see him. "She didn't know I was coming. I'll only stay a few minutes. I need to tell her something."

"Well, come on in. We're in the living room."

I kick off my shoes and follow Roger inside. Mrs. Naulty is on the couch, teacup in hand as usual.

"You have a visitor, Grandma," Roger bellows, making sure his grandmother can hear him.

"Oh, hello, Lindy," she says. "How nice to see you. Come sit down."

I perch myself on a cushy chair close to the couch where she's sitting. On the table in front of us are a teapot and a plate of cookies.

Mrs. Naulty is always baking. She always has cookies for everyone who comes to visit. She's so nice. And I'm such a jerk for taking her money.

"Would you like tea, dear? Roger, get another cup for Lindy. Or would you rather have milk? Or juice?"

"No, tea is fine."

Roger goes to the kitchen. Mrs. Naulty asks me about school. She picks up the plate and passes it to me. I take a small cookie. It's oatmeal-raisin today.

Roger comes back, pours tea for me and tops up his grandma's cup. I wonder if he's here to tell her she's moving to an old-folks' home. When he hears what I'm about to say, he'll send her away for sure.

We make small talk for a few minutes. I eat three cookies, stalling. Roger pours me a second cup of tea. He looks at his watch.

Okay, I can take a hint. Here goes.

"The reason I came over is because…"

Then I start again. "Mrs. Naulty, you know how every Saturday when I come and do chores for you, you give me two five-dollar bills in an envelope?"

She nods.

"Well, a few weeks ago, you accidentally gave me more money than that. You accidentally put two $100 bills in the envelope."

I am talking as fast as I can so I can spit it all out before I chicken out.

"I know it was a mistake. I know you didn't mean to give me that much money. But I didn't open the envelope until I got home."

I barely pause to breathe. Roger is frowning at me.

"When I realized there was too much, I should have checked with you. But I kept the money, and I've already—"

"Hang on, Lindy," Roger interrupts. "Did Grandma not tell you about that?" He looks at Mrs. Naulty, who is sipping her tea.

"Lindy, that money was from *me*," he says. "I left it with her to give to you. I know she doesn't pay you enough for everything you do for her. I know you work hard every weekend."

Now I'm confused.

"When I talked to your mom last month, she told me you were saving for a big trip. I wanted to give you a little something extra, to help you raise money."

He turns to Mrs. Naulty. "Grandma, did you forget to tell Lindy?"

Is he saying what I think he's saying? Is he saying that I did not steal that money? That it was meant for me all along?

"Did I not tell you that, love?" Mrs. Naulty says to me. "Yes, Roger left extra money for me to give to you. I gave it to you, didn't I?"

I sort of nod and shake my head at the same time. I don't know what to say.

I've been agonizing over this for a month. I've been blackmailed. I may get kicked off my Arctic trip. And the money was meant for me all along? I don't know whether to laugh or cry.

"Thanks for double-checking, Lindy. But that money is yours to keep." Roger looks at his watch again. "Sorry to cut this short, but I have to get going."

He kisses Mrs. Naulty on the cheek before he heads out. "Don't forget our appointment tomorrow, Grandma. I'll pick you up at ten o'clock."

I sit with Mrs. N. for another fifteen minutes to be polite. Before I leave, I clean up. I wash and dry the teacups and put the leftover cookies into a cookie tin. It's the least I can do.

But as soon as I can, I get out of there and run home. I can't wait to tell Mom and Dad this crazy news!

My SUN trip is back on.

Chapter Sixteen

I'm out of breath by the time I run up the front steps.

"Mom! Dad! You are never going to guess what just happened!"

I find them in the kitchen, where I left them forty-five minutes ago. They still look serious.

"I take it things went well with Mrs. Naulty," Dad says. "What did she say?"

"Well, she didn't say much. But Roger was there, and he said that the $200 was from him."

I pause to catch my breath.

"He said he told Mrs. Naulty to give it to me. And she did. But you know how she forgets everything these days? Well, she forgot to tell me that the extra money was from Roger. So I don't need to pay her back. I didn't steal anything! I didn't *actually* do anything wrong!"

Mom and Dad don't look as happy as I feel.

"This is good news, isn't it?" I'm suddenly not sure.

"Lin, you *did* do something wrong," says Mom. "Until tonight, you didn't know that money was meant for you. You didn't check with Mrs. Naulty last month, and you should have."

Geez, Mom. Way to spoil the moment.

"Your dad and I have been talking about this while you've been out. And yes, it *is* good news that Roger gave you the money. That was very generous of him. But it doesn't change *everything*."

Dad weighs in. "There will still be consequences for your actions, Lindy."

I am terrified of what's coming next.

"Your mother and I have come up with a plan," he continues. "First of all, we've decided that you'll keep working for Mrs. Naulty and the others. You may be off the hook for the $200. But there's still the money we loaned you to meet the early-bird deadline."

"I can pay that off a lot faster now," I point out.

"We don't want you to," says Mom. "We only want twenty dollars a week. That won't change. What *will* change is what happens to the rest of your earnings."

Oh no. Here it comes.

"We want you to find a charity that helps senior citizens. At the end of each month, we want you to donate your earnings to that charity."

They tell me how some seniors are on fixed incomes, meaning they don't have a lot of money. And how it's important that I learn what a difference $200 can make to some people's lives.

Okay, so far so good. I can do that.

Then they start talking about Shanna. They tell me I have to go to the school principal, and to the police, and tell them what she did.

"But she has to leave me alone now," I argue. "I have no more secrets. She can't blackmail me anymore. Nobody needs to know about it."

"Lindy, what she did is serious," says Dad. "If Shanna can't get money from you, she'll find someone else. The school and the police need to know what she's been up to."

"But that means I'll also have to tell them the whole Mrs. Naulty story," I whine. "I'll feel like an idiot."

"That would be one of the consequences," he says. "I'll arrange a meeting with the principal and the police. Your mom and I will go with you."

So now there's only one thing left to talk about. I'm afraid to ask. But I have to know.

"What about my SUN trip?" I squeak. *Please, please, please say I can go.*

"We've talked a lot about this, Lin," says Mom.

And??

"We know that you've already faced some pretty major consequences for your actions," says Dad. "Shanna made sure of that."

I realize I'm holding my breath. Slowly, I let it out.

"Are we happy that you kept Mrs. Naulty's money without checking with her?" Mom continues. "Of course not. But the fact that you told us—and Ms. Komiuk—was the right thing to do."

"Lindy, the most serious punishment we could come up with would be to take away your SUN trip," Dad says.

I gasp. *No!*

"But we have to balance that with the fact that this trip would be an incredible educational experience for you. A once-in-a-lifetime opportunity."

I hold my breath again. This could go either way right now.

"We don't want to take that opportunity away from you," says Mom.

Before I have a chance to jump for joy, she continues.

"But the truth is, it's not up to us, Lindy. Ms. Komiuk and the SUN people also have a say in this decision."

I'm sure that means I'll be staying home this summer.

Chapter Seventeen

Dad wastes no time organizing a meeting with the school principal and a police officer. We see them on Friday—and I tell them everything.

It is horrible. And embarrassing. I feel like a rat. It's one of the worst hours of my life.

"I hope you've learned your lesson about taking advantage of senior citizens," says the cop. "Elder abuse is a serious matter."

"Yes, ma'am," I say. "I will never do anything like that again."

I'm curious about what will happen to Shanna. But I'm too scared to ask. Plus, I just want to get out of the principal's office and go home.

On Monday, at the end of the day, Shanna shows up at my locker. For once she's not demanding money. But she gets right in my face.

"Hey, Snow Queen," she says icily. "Thanks to you, I got kicked out of school today."

"Leave me alone, Shanna." I try to sound confident, but my insides are in knots.

"It was fun while it lasted, wasn't it, Penguin? And I made a bit of money, thanks to you."

"You shouldn't be here, Shanna." I slam my locker shut and slide past her.

"Move. I have to get to the Northern Discovery Club meeting."

"I'm surprised Miss Igloo lets you into her classroom after what you did to that nice old lady," she sneers. "I'm *so* sorry I won't be joining you for more thrilling talk about Eskimos and walruses."

I start to say something about her racism. Instead, I turn and walk away. Her snarky voice follows me.

"Say hello to all the other polar brains for me," she calls. "At least you won't be bragging about your loser SUN trip anymore. Since I'm pretty sure you're not going now."

I turn the corner and head to Ms. Komiuk's room. I can't hear Shanna now. And she can't see that I'm almost in tears. I'm afraid she's right about the trip.

August 1. I thought this day would never come.

So much has happened in the past few months.

The biggest news in the neighborhood is that Mrs. Naulty has moved out of her house.

It turns out that the appointment she and Roger had the day after I visited was at a retirement home. Roger wanted to see if his grandma liked it. She did, and she moved there in June.

It's in a different part of town, but I've taken the bus over to see her a few times. The place has a community kitchen for residents to use. Mrs. Naulty and I baked cookies one day. Mom was right. It's not at all like jail.

Mrs. Naulty seems happy there. She has new friends. And she won't be left alone to burn the place down.

Of course, now that Mrs. Naulty is no longer in the neighborhood, I don't work for her on Saturdays anymore. I still help Mr. Finch and Mrs. Low though. And I have a few new clients. Business is good.

I've already paid Mom and Dad the $275 I owed them. And so far, I've donated about $600 to a charity that provides meals and outings for senior citizens who live alone.

It's called Friday With Friends. And it's a great idea.

Every Friday, volunteers make a three-course dinner and organize an activity at the local community center. Other volunteers drive around and pick up elderly people who wouldn't otherwise be able to get there.

The goal is to make sure that every senior in the area has at least one healthy, hot dinner a week. And to make sure that people who live alone aren't *always* alone. Many seniors can't afford to go out for a nice dinner or to have a social night out. Fridays With Friends gives them both.

Usually, about twenty-five people come. Sometimes they play cards. One time, a choir performed. Last week, a lady did a slide show about Italy.

At the end of the night, everyone gets a snack bag filled with fruit, cookies, cheese and crackers to take home. My money helps pay for the meals and snacks.

I liked the Friday With Friends idea so much that I asked if I could also become a volunteer. The volunteer manager said yes, but because I'm under eighteen, one of my parents has to come with me. Dad and I go together every week.

I've been doing a lot of charity work since everything that happened with Shanna. The Northern Discovery Club held bake sales and car washes and sold chocolate bars and anything else we could think of to raise money for Project Northern Life.

I don't feel bad that my charity, Polar Bears Forever, didn't win the club's support. Project Northern Life is a great cause. And now I get to deliver a check to the organization, in person, while I'm in the Arctic!

I have Ms. Komiuk to thank for that. It took her a while to make a decision, but in the end she told me that being a model citizen isn't about being perfect. Sometimes, it's about knowing when you've done something wrong, admitting it and dealing with the consequences.

Right now, I'm at the airport with Mom and Dad. Claire and Asha are here too. They're so excited about my trip that they asked if they could come see me off.

When my parents aren't looking, Claire and Asha give me a pair of going-away presents—the latest issue of *Canadian Geographic* and a bag of Twizzlers.

"Very funny." I stick out my tongue.

I told them how Shanna got me to ask Ben, the cute clerk at Jazzy's convenience store, about the *Canadian Geographic* magazine so she could steal Twizzlers. They haven't stopped teasing me about it since.

I haven't seen Shanna since that day at my locker. I wish someone had made her pay me back all the money she took from me. Mostly, though, I just want to forget I ever knew her.

I see a flight attendant coming our way. I'm too young to travel alone, so she'll be my babysitter until I board the plane. *How embarrassing.* "Time to go through security," she says. The flight leaves in forty-five minutes.

Mom throws her arms around me. *Please don't cry in front of my friends*, I silently beg her.

Then it's Dad's turn. He practically crushes me. "Phone us as soon as you land," he says.

Yeah, yeah.

There's a group hug with Asha and Claire, and then I follow my flight attendant-babysitter through the security door. A scanner checks my coat, knapsack and purse. A metal detector checks me. Nothing beeps. I turn and wave.

Polar bears, here I come!

ACKNOWLEDGMENTS

Thank you to the members of my summer writing group—Susan Down, Sandra McCulloch and Alex Van Tol. Four brains are definitely better than one when working out troublesome plot points! Thank you, too, to editor Melanie Jeffs for helping me make the shift from reporter to novelist, and for teaching me how to bring out the best (or worst) in my characters. I must also acknowledge the real Mrs. Naulty, whom I haven't seen in decades, but who supplied me with warm memories—and supersized chocolate bars every Halloween.

Diane Dakers has been a print and broadcast journalist since 1991, specializing in arts reporting and science journalism. *Bad Business* is her second book for Orca. Her first book, *Homecoming*, was published in fall 2014.